For my lovely sister, Anita xxx
L.P.

For Evie and her mummy and daddy xxx
C.P.

First published 2018 by Nosy Crow Ltd
The Crow's Nest, 14 Baden Place
Crosby Row, London SE1 1YW
www.nosycrow.com

ISBN 978 1 78800 265 3 (HB)
ISBN 978 1 78800 266 0 (PB)

Nosy Crow and associated logos are trademarks
and/or registered trademarks of Nosy Crow Ltd.

Text © Lou Peacock 2018
Illustrations © Christine Pym 2018

The rights of Lou Peacock to be identified as the author and of
Christine Pym to be identified as the illustrator of this work have been asserted.

A CIP catalogue record for this book is available from the British Library.

Printed in China by Imago

Papers used by Nosy Crow are made from wood grown in sustainable forests.

10 9 8 7 6 5 4 3 2 1 (HB)
10 9 8 7 6 5 4 3 2 1 (PB)

Toby
and the
Tricky Things

Lou Peacock &
Christine Pym

Toby knew that
he was getting bigger.

He thought he might
be a **Big Boy.**

He could pour
his own milk.

He could read his own
bedtime stories.

He could even reach the snacks that Mummy said were "just for mummies".

In fact, he could do most things All By Himself. Being a Big Boy, thought Toby, was marvellous.

He was also bigger than
his little sister, Iris.

Iris was very,
very small.

And because Iris was **SO** small,
Mummy was very busy.

And this meant that, sometimes,
Toby had to do the **Tricky Things**
All By Himself.

The **Tricky Things,** Toby had to admit,
were still **Tricky,** even though
he was a **Big Boy.**

When Toby had to do up his buttons,
Mummy was too busy with Iris to help.

"I'm just putting Iris's hat on, Toby," she said.
"But you're my Big Boy. You can do things All By Yourself."

But Toby couldn't.
Those buttons really were **Too Tricky**.
And he had **Bad Buttons** all day.

When Toby had to put on his wellies,
Mummy was still too busy with Iris to help.

"I'm just settling Iris in her pram, Toby," she said.
"But you're my Big Boy. You can do things All By Yourself."

But Toby couldn't.
Those wellies really were
Too Tricky. And he had
Wrong Wellies all day.

And when it came to that
other **Tricky Thing,**
it all went very wrong indeed.

Toby began to wonder
if being a Big Boy wasn't
so marvellous after all.

He called for Mummy . . .

And Mummy fixed the **Tricky Things!**
"Mummy," said Toby, "pants and
loo paper are **Tricky Things**
and I can't do **Tricky Things**
All By Myself."

"Toby, you are such a **Big Boy** and you
can do all sorts of things **All By Yourself,**"
said Mummy, "but I am always here
to help with the **Tricky Things.**"

But then Iris started to cry
and Mummy had to go to
settle her down for her nap.

Toby was **very** cross.

"Well, if I am so good at doing things
All By Myself," he thought,
"then I will have an adventure
All By Myself too."

He packed a suitcase with Toys That Might Be Useful.
Then, when everything was ready,
he set off **All By Himself**.

Toby opened the door to the garden **All By Himself**.

He climbed

down the steps

All By Himself.

And then he sat
on the swing . . .

All

By

Himself.

Toby was soon
hungry and cold.

And it turned out that
the Toys That Might
Be Useful weren't very
useful after all.

Toby didn't feel like a
Big Boy any more.

Then, just at that moment . . .

"Toby!" said Mummy.
"There you are!"

"I don't want to be a **Big Boy** and do things
All By Myself," sniffed Toby. "I want to be a baby like Iris."
"Oh, Toby," said Mummy. "You **are** my **Big Boy.**

But however big
you are, and even when
you're **all** grown up . . .

you will **always** be my baby."

"Always?" said Toby.

"Yes," said Mummy . . .